The Hubble & Hattie imprint was launched in 2009, and is named in memory of two very special Westie sisters owned by Veloce's proprietors. Since the first book, many more have been added, all with the same objective: to be of real benefit to the species they cover; at the same time promoting compassion, understanding and respect between all animals (including human ones!)

In 2017, the first Hubble & Hattie Kids! book – *Worzel says hello! Will you be my friend?* – was published, and has subsequently been joined by the second in this series – *Worzel goes for a walk! Will you come too?* ... *The Lucky, Lucky Leaf,* the first book in the Horace & Nim series ... *The Little House that didn't have a Home* ... and now *Fierce Grey Mouse.*

Our new range of books for kids will champion the same values and standards that we've always held dear, but to the adults of the future. Children will love reading, or having these beautifully illustrated, carefully crafted publications read to them, absorbing valuable life lessons whilst being highly entertained. We've more great books already in the pipeline so remember to check out our website for details.

Other books from our Hubble & Hattie Kids! imprint

9781787111608   9781787112926   9781787113060   9781787113077

www.hubbleandhattie.com

First published March 2019 by Veloce Publishing Limited, Veloce House, Parkway Farm Business Park, Middle Farm Way, Poundbury, Dorchester, Dorset, DT1 3AR, England. Tel 01305 260068/Fax 01305 250479/email info@hubbleandhattie.com/web www. hubbleandhattie.com ISBN: 978-1-787113-12-1 UPC: 6-36847-01312-7 © Chantal Bourgonje & Veloce Publishing Ltd 2019. All rights reserved. With the exception of quoting brief passages for the purpose of review, no part of this publication may be recorded, reproduced or transmitted by any means, including photocopying, without the written permission of Veloce Publishing Ltd. Throughout this book logos, model names and designations, etc, have been used for the purposes of identification, illustration and decoration. Such names are the property of the trademark holder as this is not an official publication. Readers with ideas for books about animals, or animal-related topics, are invited to write to the publisher of Veloce Publishing at the above address. British Library Cataloguing in Publication Data – A catalogue record for this book is available from the British Library. Typesetting, design and page make-up all by Veloce Publishing Ltd on Apple Mac. Printed in India by Replika Press.

One evening, Little Grey Mouse read a fascinating book about fierce creatures.

And that night, his dreams were more exciting than usual.

When he woke up the next morning, he had an idea for a great game.

"Today, I am going to be fierce."

"I will crouch like a leopard ..."

... and roar
like a lion."

"I will pounce
like a wolf ...

... and swoop
like an eagle."

Little Grey Mouse
practised his
pouncing skills,

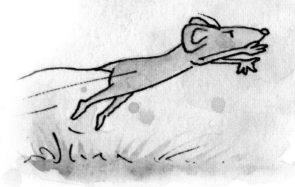

and did his
exercises

to get strong

and powerful.

He ate all his porridge

and drank all his milk.

He ruffled his
hair so it was big
and wild.

Then he put on a
ferocious stare.

OAOArRRRRRR!!!!

"I'm ready!" roared Fierce Grey Mouse.

Fierce Grey
Mouse
climbed up
the biggest
tree he
could find.

And there he sat, waiting
for someone to pounce on.

Around the corner Millie and
Pink-Nosed Rabbit were looking for
Little Grey Mouse. They wanted to
play, but he was nowhere to be seen.

Fierce Grey Mouse saw
them from his branch
high up in the tree.

"Oh, no! What's that?"
cried Millie.

Fierce Grey Mouse
roared.

Millie and Pink-Nosed Rabbit ran and hid
behind a tree.

All day long Fierce Grey Mouse roared and pounced on everyone he saw.

But after
a while
no one
came by
anymore.

They were all too scared.

Fierce Grey Mouse felt lonely.

"Is anybody there?" he cried out.

But nobody answered.

Being fierce wasn't much fun anymore. He smoothed down his wild fur.

He softened his ferocious stare.

"Hello," Little Grey Mouse called out, with his Little Grey Mouse voice.

"Would anyone like to play?"

Millie and Pink-Nosed
Rabbit peeped out from
behind the tree.

"Watch out,
Little Grey
Mouse!

There is something
fierce about!" And they
hid behind the tree
again.

"But that was me!" squeaked Little Grey Mouse with his Little Grey Mouse voice.

"Really?" asked Millie and Pink-Nosed Rabbit.

"Yes, it was really me. Can we play again?"

"No roaring or swooping or pouncing?" they asked.

"I promise," said Little Grey Mouse. "Just playing and having fun with friends."

And that's exactly
what they did.